Judy Moody
and the Bucket List

Judy Moody

and the
Bucket List

Megan McDonald

illustrated by
Peter H. Reynolds

CANDLEWICK PRESS

official stuff

Text copyright © 2016 by Megan McDonald
Illustrations copyright © 2016 by Peter H. Reynolds
Judy Moody font copyright © 2003 by Peter H. Reynolds
Judy Moody®. Judy Moody is a registered trademark of Candlewick Press, Inc.

First paperback edition in this format 2018

Library of Congress Catalog Card Number 2015940257
ISBN 978-0-7636-7995-8 (hardcover)
ISBN 978-1-5362-0082-9 (paperback)

18 19 20 21 22 23 BVG 10 9 8 7 6 5 4 3 2 1

Printed in Berryville, VA, U.S.A.

This book was typeset in Stone Informal and Judy Moody.
The illustrations were done in watercolor, tea, and ink.

Candlewick Press
99 Dover Street
Somerville, Massachusetts 02144

visit us at www.candlewick.com

Table of Contents

Kick-the-Bucket List...................... 1

Electrikitty............................14

Antarctica or Bust 27

Izzy Azumi, F.D.O....................40

Can²tractions 52

Drums Up!.............................66

Bucket-List Buddies...................85

The Dud Ranch 97

HypnoToady..........................118

Do Not/Don't-Kick-the-Bucket List 139

Judy Moody

Queen of the Bucket List

Dad

Former Electric Drumsticks
Band Member

Mom

Ouchless Hairbrush
Enthusiast

Stink

aka HypnoToady

Who's Who

Izzy Azumi

F.D.O. (Future Dog Owner)

Mouse

Hepcat

Grandma Lou

Bucket-List Buddy

Kick-the-Bucket List

Sunflower seeds. Sharpie. Superglue. She, Judy Moody, was pawing through Grandma Lou's purse. Her bag was like a treasure chest. A treasure chest with snaps and zippers and hidden pockets and secret compartments.

"Grandma Lou," Judy called, "I can't find the cards. We can't play Go Fish without a deck of cards."

"Keep looking," Grandma Lou called

back. "Bring me my reading glasses, too, please."

Knitting, mini-flashlight, granola bar, cough drops, cards. Cards! Judy held up the deck. But finding glasses in Grandma Lou's purse was like a game of Go Fish.

While Judy was fishing around in the purse, she just happened to notice a folded piece of paper sticking out of an inside pocket.

It was probably just a shopping list that said *carrots* and *toilet paper*. But it didn't look scribbly. It had for-real handwriting in cursive. Maybe it wasn't a shopping list. What if it was a treasure map? Or a love letter? Maybe Grandma Lou had a secret pen pal.

Judy sneak-peeked a look at the paper. It was a list! But NOT a boring-old shopping list. Grandma Lou's list said *Bucket List* at the top. What in the world was a bucket list?

Judy was often in a list-making mood herself. She even had a list of her lists:

- Nicknames to call Stink
- Christmas list on toilet paper
- Bummer Summer list of dares

Maybe Grandma Lou liked lists, too. Same-same!

Louise M. Moody's Bucket List
- Ride an elephant
- See the pyramids in Egypt
- ~~Send a message in a bottle~~

- Gaze at the northern lights
- Sleep in a castle
- ~~Swim with dolphins~~
- Learn sign language
- Make a difference
- Dance the rumba
- Read *War and Peace* for the third time

Judy rushed over to Grandma Lou. She held the list behind her back.

"Grandma Lou," said Judy, "if a person just happened to be looking in another person's purse, and she just happened to find something interesting, would it be okay for that person to ask the other person about it even if it's personal?"

"Ask away," said Grandma Lou.

Judy dangled the paper in front of Grandma Lou. "I found a list that doesn't say *toothpaste* or *carrots and toilet paper*. It says *Bucket List* and it has way-cool stuff on it like *Ride an elephant*. What's a bucket list?" Judy asked.

"A bucket list is . . . " Grandma Lou started. "Well, see, a bucket list . . . " Grandma Lou was biting her bottom lip. That meant she was thinking about how to explain it. "It's like a wish list."

A wish list! Judy wanted to make a wish list, too. Judy wanted to ride an elephant!

"But why not just call it a wish list? Why call it a bucket list?"

"It's a special kind of wish list. A list

of all the things I'd like to do before I . . .
you know. Kick the bucket."

Judy could not believe her ears or eyes!

Kick. The. Bucket. As in croak. As in
bite the dust, give up the ghost, take a
dirt nap.

Gulp. Judy did not want to think the
thought. She put her head on Grandma
Lou's shoulder. "Grandma Lou, you're
not going to, um, die, are you?"

"Well, someday, but not anytime soon. Don't you worry, Jelly Bean. I'm going to be around for a good long time. But there's a lot I'd like to do before that time comes. So I started a list."

"Phew," said Judy, letting out the breath she'd been holding. She could not imagine her life without Grandma Lou in it.

Wait just a kick-the-bucket second. Judy liked lists. Judy was the Queen of Lists. She, Judy Moody, would make her own list. Her very own kick-the-bucket list of all the stuff she wanted to do before she . . . went to fourth grade!

Judy tore out a piece of notebook paper. She chewed the end of her pencil.

She chewed it some more.

"That pencil's beginning to look like a shark attacked it," said Grandma Lou.

"Shark attack!" said Stink, running into the room. "What? Where?"

"It's just my pencil, Stink." Judy held out her classic No. 2 Grouchy pencil.

Stink examined it under the magnifying glass. "Yep. This looks like the work of a Japanese goblin shark. For sure."

Judy held out her hand. "Give it. I have a V.I.L. to make. Very Important List."

"V.I.B.L.," said Stink. "Very Important Bucket List."

"Hey, how did you —?" Judy squinted a

stink-eye at her brother. "You were spying on us this whole time!"

"I spy with my little eye . . . something yellow, with words, on notebook paper."

"My bucket list!" said Judy.

He handed back the pencil, squeezing in next to Judy on the couch. He pretended to read his *Big Head Book of Scat*.

"Need some help?" Grandma Lou asked Judy.

Judy nodded. "How did you know what to put on your list?" she asked.

"Let's see. First I dreamed of places I'd like to go. Then I thought about new things I might want to learn."

Judy scribbled a few ideas on her list.

"Write down 'Smell a corpse flower,'" said Stink.

"P.U.," said Judy.

"Write down 'Sleep with a shark,'" said Stink.

"We already did that," said Judy. "At the aquarium."

"Write down 'Invent something,'" said Stink. Judy wrote it down so Stink would stop bugging her.

"Just use your imagination," said Grandma Lou. "Dream a little. And follow your heart."

Judy scribbled a few more ideas. She covered her paper with her arm so Stink couldn't spy on her. At last she

was done. Ta-da! Her way-official not-yet-fourth-grade kick-the-bucket bucket list.

Judy decided to go fish one more time in Grandma Lou's purse. She pulled out a granola bar and took a bite. A big bite. A Japanese-goblin-shark-size bite.

She was going to need tons of energy for her big bucket-list adventure. She couldn't wait to get started. Judy tried to turn a cartwheel down the hall, but she flopped and landed, plop, on the floor. No worries. Learning to cartwheel was on her list. A few more shark-bites of energy bar and she would be on her way.

Electrikitty

The next day, Judy went to find Mom. Mom was on the back deck, painting a chair blue.

"Mom?" Judy asked. "Can I ride a horse or go to camp or see all of London from the tippy-top of the London Eye?"

Mom did not even look up from her painting. "Ask your father."

Judy went to find Dad. Dad was under

the kitchen sink, fixing a pipe. "Hey, Dad, can I ride a horse or go to camp or see all of London—"

Dad did not even pop his head out. "Go ask your mother," he said before Judy could finish her sentence.

Sheesh. Weren't moms and dads supposed to listen to their kids?

Judy went out to the back deck. She sat on a bench, her head bent, studying her kick-the-bucket list. *Cartwheel, invention, triple stickers . . .*

Her hair fell down over her face in a tangle. "Judy," Mom said, finally looking up, "remember when you were in a good mood for a whole week and you brushed your hair every day? I liked that week."

Judy pointed to the mangle of tangles in her hair. "Show me a hairbrush that doesn't hurt, and I'll show you hair that is brushed."

Lightbulb! She, Judy Moody, could not believe her own genius idea. A brush that doesn't hurt! On her bucket list, it said *Invent something.* She, Judy Moody, would invent . . . the Ouchless Hairbrush. No more knots. No more hurt. Who wouldn't want one?

"Never mind about camp," she said to Mom. She raced upstairs. Mouse was sitting on her brush. "Move it, Mouse," she told her cat.

Judy grabbed her hairbrush and pulled all the cat hair off of it first. She stared at the spikes sticking up out of her brush. So many spikes. No wonder hairbrushes were such a pain. Her brush was half porcupine!

Judy tried to yank the brush through her hair. *Youch!* Attack of the Porcupine!

If porcupines had thirty thousand spiny quills, Judy's brush must have had at least *three* thousand spiky bristles.

All she had to do was to get rid of all the hurty spikes. *Pop! Pop! Pop!* One by one, she popped out all the bristles.

Wa-la! The Ouchless Hairbrush was born. No more porcupine! From now on, every day was Be Kind to Your Hair Day.

Judy deserved to award herself a Bright Idea sticker for this invention. She would call it . . . the Spineless Porcupine. The Porcu-pineless. The Porcu-*pain*less.

Judy could not wait to show off her new invention. First to her family, then the world! She could already see the head-lines:

BREAKING NEWS

PORCUPAINLESS SWEEPS THE NATION!

INVENTOR JUDY MOODY

INNOVATIONS

OUCHLESS HAIRBRUSH

GREATEST INVENTION SINCE BUBBLE GUM

MOVE OVER, TRAMPOLINE!
MELT DOWN, POPSICLE!
MAKE WAY FOR...
PORCUPAINLESS!

Showtime. Judy gathered her family on the couch, including Mouse. Mouse curled up on her mood pillow. Her invention sat on the coffee table, covered with a dish towel. But even a dish towel could not hide its genius. It was practically pulsing with possibility. And Judy was popping with pride.

19

Mom and Dad sat on the couch. Stink sat on the edge of his seat.

"Stink, tell me when it's five o'clock. At five o'clock on the dot, we will have the unveiling."

Stink watched his watch. Mom looked sleepy. Dad seemed to be distracted. Stink counted down the seconds. "Five, four, three, two, one!"

Judy wished she had a drum for a drumroll. She tried to make it sound exciting. "Mr. President. Mrs. President. Ladies and Germs." She looked right at Stink. "Today, I present to you the World's Newest Invention, from the brain of an eight-year-old girl in Virginia." Judy took a deep breath. She reached down and pulled off the towel.

"Ta-da!" said Judy, sweeping her arms through the air and pointing to her invention with a grand gesture.

"Is that some kind of newfangled Ping-Pong paddle?" Dad asked.

"What happened to your brush?" Mom asked.

Stink just stared. "So your invention is . . . the Naked Hairbrush?"

"No! Guys, guys. You don't get it. Allow me to demonstrate." Judy took another deep breath. "Behold the amazing, the never-before-seen, the ultimate . . . are you ready? Presenting . . . the Ouchless

Hairbrush! I call it the Porcu*pain*less!"

Judy stopped and stared at her family. They were quiet. Too quiet.

They must be stunned into silence with amazement!

Wait till they saw this. "Now, I'll show you the Porcupainless in action!" *Wa-la!* She picked up the brush and ran it across her hair. Of course, without any bristles, it didn't *really* brush her hair. But it didn't hurt or yank or pull either!

"What do you think?" she asked her family.

"I think you made your hair stand up on end!" said Stink, cracking up.

Judy touched the top of her head.

She ran and looked at herself in the hall mirror. Stink was right. Her hair was sticking up. Straight up! She looked like a dandelion puffball. She looked like a Chia Pet.

"You know, Edison tried thousands of times before getting the lightbulb right," said Dad.

"I'm sure Ben Franklin didn't invent the lightning rod in a day," said Mom.

Mom and Dad were just being Mom and Dad—saying nice parent stuff so Judy wouldn't feel bad.

Stink held up his *Big Head Book of Inventions.* "And I'm sure it took Margaret Knight *tons* of time to invent the square-bottom paper bag."

Judy looked her brother in the eyes. "Stink, tell me the truth. Isn't the Ouch-less Hairbrush a good invention?"

Stink squirmed like a worm. "Um, well, maybe you could just change the name a little," said Stink. "You could call it the Electro-Magnetron or something."

"Or something," said Judy. She collapsed in an un-cartwheel heap on the floor. Mouse leaped into her lap.

"At least Mouse likes it," said Judy. She brushed the Ouchless Hairbrush along her cat's back. Judy got a shock of static electricity. Mouse's hair stood straight up like a scaredy-cat cartoon kitty.

"She looks like a

porcupine!" said Stink. Judy and Stink cracked up.

"Instead of electricity, she's Electri-kitty!" said Judy.

"The Ouchless Hairbrush," yelled Stink, "turns any ordinary cat into Bride of Frankenstein."

"The Ouchless Hairbrush," said Judy, "puts a spark in your hair *and* your cat."

She sprang up and hurried upstairs. "That's it!"

"Wait. Where are you going?" asked Stink.

"To invent a shampoo that will get rid of static electricity," said Judy. "I'll call it . . . the Electrikitty Anti-Static Pet Hair Neutralizer." *Purr-fect!*

Antarctica or Bust

Judy misted Mouse with her purr-fect cat spray. (Water plus oil-spill-approved dish soap.) She crossed *Invent something* off her bucket list. Her eyes fell on the words *Go to Antarctica*.

Judy poked her head into Stink's room. "Hey, Stink, how much do you think it costs to go to Antarctica?"

"I don't know. One flunked spelling test? Two not-turned-in homeworks?

Three times interrupting Mr. Todd when he's talking?"

"Not *that* Antarctica." Stink thought she was talking about the desk in the back of Class 3T where you had to go to Chill Out. "The *real* one."

"Oh. Let's see. More than you have in your piggy bank."

"Ha! I bet you didn't know I have thirty-three dollars and forty-one cents saved up."

"It costs thirty-three *gazillion* dollars to go to Antarctica. You'd need forty-one winter coats, too."

The air went out of Judy. She slumped onto Stink's bed like a sock monkey that had lost its stuffing.

"It's super far away, you know. Farther than it is to go to Santa's house at the North Pole." Stink spun his light-up globe and pointed to a continent at the bottom of the world that was shaped like a heart with one wing. "It's all the way down here at the South Pole."

Judy searched her wildest imagination. "So maybe five hundred dollars?"

"More."

"Seven hundred?"

"More. Because they just found a giant squid down there that weighs seven-hundred seventy pounds and is as big as a minibus. Tons of people are going to want to go see it, so it will probably cost more now."

"A *thousand?*" said Judy. Stink nodded.

Sheesh! One thousand dollars. That was a lot of scratch. Bones. Bread. Dough. Moola! She'd better get started right away if she had even a slim chance of raising that many dead presidents by the fourth grade!

That night after dinner, Judy called everybody back to the couch. Emergency Family Meeting time. Stink looked around for another mystery lump under a dish towel. But he didn't see any Judy inventions.

"What is it this time?" he asked. "The Ouchless Band-Aid? The De-Electrifying Toothbrush?"

"Ha-ha. Very funny, Stink. I called

you all here to ask for a raise in my allowance."

"No," said Mom and Dad.

"No," said Stink.

"Not you, Stink." Judy gave him the not-ouchless hairy eyeball stare. "You haven't even heard my reasons. I have a whole speech and everything."

"You just *got* a raise, Jelly Bean," said Dad. Judy hated it when Dad said no and called her *Jelly Bean* at the same time. It was so not fair.

"She already got fifty more cents last month," said Stink.

"Thanks a lot, Stinkbug," said Judy. For a little brother, Stink sure had a big mouth. "You may be excused, Stink, if you want to go to your room."

"I'm fine here," said Stink.

Plan B. "Okay, what if I did some chores for some extra money. I could unload the dishwasher sometimes. Or I could maybe put away my own laundry pile without anybody telling me."

"That's what the fifty cents was for!" piped up Stink.

"Stink's right," Mom pointed out. "You're already supposed to be doing those things."

"Fine," said Judy. Time for Plan C.

Judy made a poster-board sign that said ANTARCTICA OR BUST! She drew a thermometer. At the bottom she wrote $33.41. At the top she wrote $1,000 big ones.

She sat on the curb for half of Sunday with a bucket for money. She told everybody who passed by about her bucket list. She told them she was accepting donations for a worthy cause: Antarctica!

She could not wait to start coloring her thermometer in red. But at the end of the morning, all she had was two dimes, a Canadian penny, a paper clip, and a linty cough drop.

Roar! She, Judy Moody, was in a mood, until . . . Stink hired her to pick up his Snappos. One whole dollar bill for picking

up ten bazillion Snappos off the living room floor! And it was not even part of Plan A, B, or C.

Plan D, here I come!

Judy knocked on some doors around the neighborhood: 119 Croaker Road, no answer; 121 Croaker, no answer; 123 Croaker, Mrs. Soso was home!

"Hi, Mrs. Soso," said Judy. "I was wondering, um . . . " Judy looked around the yard, trying to think of a way to make a little money. No dandelions to pull. No leaves to rake. "See, I'm saving for a trip to Antarctica, and . . . maybe I could search for four-leaf clovers in your yard? They're good luck, you know. And if I find one, you could pay me a dollar."

"No, thanks. I'm good," said Mrs. Soso.

Judy looked around some more. There was a big willow tree in the side yard. "I could climb that tree and tell you what it looks like from up there. Maybe there's a bird's nest. Or a squirrel's nest. That would only cost you seventy-five cents."

"Tell you what," said Mrs. Soso. "You could scoop up the dog poop in the front yard."

Judy's nose itched. Judy's nose twitched just thinking about it. *P.U.!* Getting to Antarctica was not going to be easy. But it *was* on her bucket list. Even if it meant scooping poop, she was up for it. Judy Moody, Pooper Scooper, to the rescue!

Judy got a tiny shovel and a plastic bag. With each scoop of poop, she tried to count penguins. Anything but poop. Antarctica was full of penguins. Emperor penguins, gentoo penguins, macaroni penguins . . .

Just then, Rocky and Frank saw Judy from across the street. Rocky was walking Houdini (his pet iguana) and Frank was walking the dog (his pet yo-yo).

"Hey, Judy!" Rocky called, waving.

"Whatcha doing?" Frank asked.

"What's it look like?" Judy asked. "I'm pooping scoop."

Rocky and Frank cracked up. Judy cracked up, too. "I mean scooping poop."

"What for?" asked Frank.

"For money. I need some scratch-moola-cashola, and fast." Judy explained all about Antarctica and her bucket list.

"We'd help, but it's a super-stinky job," said Rocky, holding his nose.

"I'll help," said Frank.

"Thanks, but this is really a one-pooper-scooper town."

"Want to come with Frank and me to Fur & Fangs?" Rocky asked.

Judy looked over the rest of the yard. She hated to be a party pooper, but every piece of poop was like a dollar sign. "Can't," said Judy. "More poop to scoop!"

King penguins, little blue penguins, rock-hopper penguins . . .

Izzy Azumi, F.D.O.

Stink came and peered over Mrs. Soso's fence at the bag of poop that Judy had scooped. "Whoa. Where's the moose?" he asked.

"Huh?" said Judy.

"That's moose poop if I ever saw it," said Stink.

"How do you know it's moose poop?" asked Judy.

"It's too big to be dog poop. Looks more

like cow plop. I'm reading *The Big Head Book of Scat* from the library. I'm kind of a scat expert, you know."

It was true-not-false. Stink did know a lot about scat and poop and dung. "Moose poop, huh?" said Judy, with a gleam in her eye. Cha-ching! She should make *even more* money for scooping poop that size. "Scooping moose poop has to be worth way more than dog poop. Maybe even five big ones."

"At least," said Stink.

When Judy was done, she knocked on Mrs. Soso's front door to collect her money. As it turned out, it was only worth five little-not-big ones. Five dimes. A puny fifty cents.

"How much did you get?" Stink asked. Judy held out her hand.

"Fifty cents? That's all?" said Stink. "That's dog poop."

"Exactly," said Judy. "Mrs. Soso says poop is poop."

"Bummer," said Stink, hopping down off the fence. "Gotta go. I'm late for a thumb-wrestling match with Webster."

"See you later!" said Judy.

Stink was halfway down the sidewalk when he turned around. "You know what you need? *Polar bear* scat. Now *that's* worth something."

"Now you tell me," said Judy.

Gold mine! If Stink was right, she could scoop poop from possums to pot-bellied pigs, elk to emus. The bigger the better. She'd make piles of money. Heaps of it. Mountains of money.

Judy knocked on three more doors. Not one person wanted their possum poop scooped. And nobody even owned an emu.

On the way home, Judy kept an eye out for polar bear scat. "I'm Linda Gormezano, Polar Bear Poop Tracker," she said aloud. Stink had read to Judy all about Linda Gormezano from his *Big Head Book of Scat*. "For five dollars, I'll track down your polar bear poop and scoop it!"

All of a sudden, Judy saw a pair of striped kneesocks sticking out from a

pair of polka-dot rubber boots. They belonged to a girl with freckles who was holding a leash and who seemed to be walking an invisible dog.

"Hi, Linda," said a voice. "I'm Izzy. Izzy Azumi, F.D.O."

"Oh, no, I was just pretending," said Judy. "I'm not Linda. I'm Judy. Judy Moody, P.B.P.T."

"P.B.P.T.? Oh, Polar Bear . . . Poop Tracker?" Izzy asked.

"Yep," said Judy. "And F.D.O.? Fire Drill Organizer? Fluffy Dog Oilpainter? Fried Donut Operator?"

Izzy shook her head no, no, and no. She cracked up, showing two missing teeth.

"Freaky-Deaky *Octopus?*" asked Judy. "I give up. I'm all out of stuff with the letter *O.*"

"Future Dog Owner!" said Izzy, breaking into more giggles.

"Is that why you're walking an invisible dog?" Judy asked.

"Uh-huh. I'm practicing for someday when there's a real puppy at the end of this leash."

"I'd shake your hand or something, but I might smell like poop," said Judy. She explained all about her poop-scooping job.

"Someday soon I'll be scooping poop, too. I'm going to get a dog. A cockapoo puppy. They're really fuzzy. And funny.

Animal Planet says they're surprisingly human."

"I love cockapoos!" said Judy. "Do you live around here?"

"My dad does," said Izzy. "Most times I live with my mom, but on weekends I stay with my dad. Me and my brother do."

"Brothers," said Judy. "Don't get me started."

"I know, right?" said Izzy.

"Hey, Izzy. I'm trying to make some money for a trip to Antarctica. So if you ever need your invisible dog walked, I'm the girl for the job. Or if you need me to scoop any cockapoo poop, it'll only cost you fifty cents."

A kid on a skateboard came zooming

down the sidewalk. "Yikes. Here comes my brother, Ian. I'll give you fifty cents right now not to say anything about the F.D.O. He'll just make fun of me and tell me I'm never going to get a dog."

Shush money! Money just for keeping a secret. This was even better than poop scooping.

"I'm a good secret keeper," said Judy. Izzy thrust the leash into Judy's hand.

Izzy's brother and his skateboard came to a stop outside the fence. He upended the board, showing off an alien and the words *CANDY RIOT*, along with bright-orange trucks and neon-green wheels.

"Dad was wondering where you were,"
said Ian.

"I'm just talking to my new friend."
Izzy put her hands in the air and cartwheeled right across Judy's front lawn.

Bing! Cartwheel! Meeting Izzy Azumi,
F.D.O., could be a bucket-list moment.

"Later." Ian shook his head and sped off down the sidewalk.

"Hey, Izzy," said Judy. "You know the fifty cents you were going to pay me to keep your secret?"

"Uh-huh."

"If you teach me to do a cartwheel," Judy offered, "we'll call it even, okay?"

"One handed or two?" Izzy asked.

"Two!" said Judy.

Izzy told her it was easy-peasy. "All you have to do is remember H.H.F.F."

"Hop, Hop, Fall, Fall?" Judy asked.

"Hand, Hand, Foot, Foot. Like this." Izzy raised her hands in the air. Izzy put one hand on the ground, then the other.

She lifted off one foot and, in a blink, she twirled through the air.

Judy watched. Judy waited. Judy tried. *Crash! Plunk! Pfft!* Judy landed on her you-know-what. Turning cartwheels was so *not* easy-peasy. Turning cartwheels was a B.L.B., Bucket-List Bummer.

Can'tractions

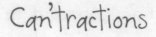

Antarctica? Nope. Cartwheel? Nope. *Rats!* Judy could not check either of these off her kick-the-bucket list yet. She wrote *Meet girl with invisible dog* on her list and crossed it off. That put her in a better bucket-list mood.

Judy scanned her list. *Get triple stickers on homework.* How hard could it be to get not one, not two, but *three* stickers for good work? Three stickers was triple good. Three stickers was tops. Three stickers was the trifecta of Mr. Todd stickers. *Excelente! Qué bien! Perfecto!*

Jessica Finch had gotten three Bright Idea lightbulbs. Jessica Finch had gotten Top Cat, Cool Cat, and Cat's Meow. But even Jessica Finch had not gotten every one of the triple-sticker sets in Mr. Todd's top desk drawer.

Judy took out her homework. *Eek!* She had not done her homework all week. She stared at the no-sticker homework sheets. She imagined *Home Run! Grand Salami! Moonshot!* dancing at the top of the page. *Perfecto!*

All she had to do was work extra hard. She circled homophones. She learned heaps of helping verbs. She was a synonym sleuth. She unscrambled names of all the desert plants. She filled out her loggerhead turtle fact sheet.

She saved contractions for last. Contractions were baby stuff. Kid stuff. Second-grade stuff. *Can't go wrong! Won't fail! Couldn't be better!*

At school on Monday, Judy could hardly wait until Mr. Todd passed back their homework sheets. At last it was time. Triple sticker time! Judy crossed all eight fingers and both thumbs.

"Class 3T," said Mr. Todd, clearing his throat. *Uh-oh.* Clearing his throat was never good, unless Mr. Todd had his guitar and was about to sing. But Judy did not see a guitar. And that frown was not part of his singing face.

He started to pass back the contractions homework. Judy could picture it now. Three stickers in a row: *Smarty Pants! Wizard! Fourth Grade Here I Come!*

What!? Judy stared wide-eyed at her homework. She was seeing red! Instead of seeing three stickers, she saw red, red, red.

Triple *red* trifecta. The page looked like it was covered in ketchup. The page looked like it was bleeding and needed a giant Band-Aid. The page was as messed up as a spaghetti sandwich.

Mr. Todd was saying, "People. People. What went wrong here? Contractions are just a review. I happen to know you learned this in second grade."

Frank tried to say they *hadn't* learned contractions. Rocky tried to say they *didn't* remember. Judy tried to say they *couldn't* fit any more stuff in their third-grade brains, because fractions were taking three-fourths of the room in there.

Mr. Todd said, "No excuses." Mr. Todd said they had to do their homework over again. Mr. Todd said, "How will you make it in fourth grade if you don't know contractions?"

Grr! Judy stared at her paper. She *couldn't, wouldn't, didn't* get one single sticker. Contractions made Judy itch. Contractions made Judy squirm. All those apostrophes! Who knew where they went?

They should be called *can'tractions!*

If I can't learn contractions, I won't ever go to fourth grade!

Judy asked Frank for help. Frank had more red marks than she did! She asked Jessica Finch next. "I'll help, but then you have to call me Queen of Contractions," said Jessica. *Roar!*

Lightbulb! Suddenly, she, Judy Moody, had a bright idea. All she needed was a hall pass.

Judy raised her hand. "Mr. Todd," she said, "*I* apostrophe *D* like to be excused." *I'd. I* apostrophe *D.* Good one. She should receive one lightbulb sticker just for that.

Judy hightailed it down the hall to Room 2D. Stink's room. Stink was her brainstorm. Stink was her bright idea. Stink was her ticket to a *Home Run*!

Stink was in second grade. Stink knew an easy way to remember contractions. He was always driving her cuckoo with some crazy song about contractions.

Psst! Judy motioned to her brother from

the doorway. "Hi, Mrs. D." Judy waved. "May I borrow my brother for a sec?"

Stink shook his head no, but Mrs. D. nodded yes.

When Stink came to the door, Judy pulled him into the hall. "Stinkbug. You gotta help me. Quick. Tell me everything you know about contractions."

"Can't," said Stink.

"Ha-ha, very funny," said Judy.

"No, I mean it. Right now Mrs. D. is reading us fables, and we get to guess the morals. I love morals. I don't want to miss any."

"Morals, schmorals," said Judy.

"Can't you come back when we do base ten this afternoon?"

"No, Stinker. I can't."

"*Can't?* Or *won't?*"

"C'mon, Stink. It's a matter of life and fourth grade!"

Judy and Stink sat on top of the heater at the end of the hallway. "Teach me that song you always sing about contractions." Judy checked the clock. "You have five minutes. Go."

"But you hate that song. You said —"

"Forget whatever I said. Sing!"

"Just so you know, it goes to the tune of 'London Bridge Is Falling Down.' And it helps you figure out where to put the contraction when you combine two words. I mean the apostrophe thingie."

"Got it," said Judy.

Stink started singing:

"I'm the first word, don't change me!

Don't change me, don't change me.

I'm the first word, don't change me!

Please just let me be."

"Don't got it," Judy said.

"Wait, I'm not done," Stink told her. He sang the second verse:

"When you change the second word,

Second word, second word,

When you change the second word,

Use an a-pos-tro-phe!

"Now you sing it," said Stink.

Judy sang, *"Now you got me all con-fused, all con-fused, all con-fused . . . "*

"Okay, look. Like the song says, never change the first word. If the words you're combining are *can* and *not,* you never change *can.* You always put the apostrophe in the second word, in place of the missing letters."

Just then, the principal walked past. "Judy, Stink," said Ms. Tuxedo, "shouldn't you be in class?"

"Yes," said Judy, "but we *are* learning. I'm . . . helping Stink with contractions."

"I'm helping *her!*" Stink protested.

"I have to admit," said Ms. Tuxedo, "when it comes to contractions, *they're* tricky." She winked at Judy.

Judy wondered why she winked. Then—duh—it hit her. Right in the middle of her third-grade brain.

"I get it! *They're* is not *there* or *their. They're* is a contraction."

Judy hummed the song to herself. "Wait, don't tell me. *They're* is short for *they are.*" She hummed some more. She remembered what Stink told her. Never change the first word.

"*They* stays the same. Drop the *a* in the second word and *are* becomes apostrophe *r-e. T-h-e-y* apostrophe *r-e.*" It was all coming back to her now.

"That's correct!" said Ms. Tuxedo.

"*That's* is a contraction for *that is. That* apostrophe *s.*"

"Beautiful," said Ms. Tuxedo.

"See, Stink? That *wasn't* so hard. *Wasn't. W-a-s-n* apostrophe *t.*"

"But I — you — never mind. Know anything about base ten?" Stink asked Ms. Tuxedo.

Judy skipped off down the hall, singing all the way. She slid into her seat, pulled out her homework, and fixed all the contractions. This time, Judy's homework did not need a giant Band-Aid. London Bridge was not falling down after all.

She should get a *trophy* for all those apos-*trophes!* But *she would/she'd* be happy with a triple-sticker trifecta. Bingo! Then she could cross it off her bucket list.

Awesome sauce! Awesome sandwich! Awesome-sauce banana peel!

Drums Up!

The next day, Mr. Todd handed back the homework do-overs. He was wearing his Proud-of-Class-3T face. "I knew *you would/ you'd* turn this around," he said. "Good work, 3T."

Judy *could not/couldn't* believe her eyes. Triple stickers! Were her eyes playing tricks on her?

Judy showed off her homework to Rocky and Frank. Their eyes bugged out of their heads. "Awesome-sauce banana peel?" said Frank. "*That is/that's* like the best of all the triple stickers!"

Rocky agreed. "You *cannot/can't* get any better than that. *You are/you're* like the Queen of Contractions."

"Thanks!" said Judy, hoping Jessica Finch heard that one. She drew a picture of an apostrophe trophy and gave it to herself. Then she took out her bucket list and crossed off *Get triple stickers on homework.*

That's when *Learn a musical instrument* caught her eye. She had an awesome-sauce after-school idea.

As soon as the last bell rang, Judy

followed Frank and his tuba down the hall to the music room. He filled Judy in on the way.

"Mr. Nulty is the music teacher."

"Got it," said Judy.

"He's really nutty about music."

"Uh-huh."

"But whatever you do, don't call him Mr. Nutty," said Frank.

"Got it," said Judy.

"Hi, Mr. Nulty," Frank called. "This is my friend Judy. Can we look around? Judy wants to play an instrument."

"Great!" said Mr. Nulty. "Music should be a part of everyone's life, right, Frank?"

"Right, Mr. Nutty," said Frank. *Oops!* "I mean Nulty."

"If you want to play," Mr. Nulty told Judy, "you have to come once a week after school for a twenty-two-minute lesson. And you'll need to give up one recess a week to come play. How does that sound?"

"Good," said Judy. Mr. Nulty handed her a permission slip to get signed.

There were instruments all over the music room—on desks, on tables, on stands. Big brass horns and tiny, shiny flutes and violins with strings.

"Go ahead. Take a look around," said Mr. Nulty. "What do you think you might want to play?" He held up a French horn and played a few bars from the theme to *Star Wars*.

"Ooh-la-la!" said Judy.

He held up a saxophone and played a riff from "Take Me Out to the Ballgame."

"Snazzy and jazzy," said Judy.

Then he played some high sweet notes on the flute.

"I like pressing buttons!" said Judy.

The room was almost spinning. Her head was a symphony of sounds. "They all sound so good. How will I ever decide?" said Judy, twirling and untwirling a squiggle of hair around her finger.

"Pick one up. Try it out," said Mr. Nulty. "Don't be shy. I have to run to the office and make some copies. I'll give you a few minutes. Frank here can help you."

Frank held up a flute. "Here. Everybody likes the flute. Try this one."

Judy held the flute to her lips. She blew into the mouthpiece. *Eek! Squeak!*

"It sounds like a mouse!" Judy said. Frank cracked up.

She picked up the sax. *Awk! Squawk!* It sounded like a pet-store parrot.

"How about the trombone?" said Frank, making a sliding motion with his hand.

Judy tried the trombone. She blew into the end of the slide. *Pfft!* All that came out was spit. She moved the slide and tried again. *Pfft!* More spit! She tried one more time. Spit flew across the room.

"Play it, don't spray it," Frank teased.

When Judy tried the clarinet, it let out a sneeze. When she tried the French horn, it wheezed. She said "Oh, no" to the oboe. She said "Lump it" to the trumpet.

At last, Frank held out his tuba. "Here, try the tuba. I'm telling you—it's really fun. I'll show you."

"But it's bigger than me!" said Judy.

"The great part is that you can sit down while you play," said Frank. He sat down and played "My Hat, It Has Three Corners."

"Hey! That's good!" said Judy.

"Your turn," said Frank. He showed her how to hold it in her lap. He showed her where to put her fingers. "Now, fill your cheeks with air and blow into this tube."

Judy sat with the tuba in her lap. She put her fingers on the buttons. Frank got ready to give her a big thumbs-up!

She blew.

Moo! Mooooo! It sounded like a cow. "My hat, it has three cows," said Judy. They *could not/couldn't* help cracking up.

Pretty soon, Judy had tried nearly

every instrument in the room. So far, all they did was *eek, moo,* cough, and sneeze. Not one note. Not one musical sound.

"Forget it," Judy said to Frank. "I'll kick the bucket for real before I ever get to cross this off my kick-the-bucket list!"

"There has to be *something* here you can play," said Frank, looking around. "Hey! How about the triangle!"

"Hello! Preschool! Everybody knows the triangle is for babies."

Just then, Mr. Nulty came back from the office. "How's it going?" he asked.

"Not so great," said Judy. "Did you know your clarinet has a cold?" She picked up the French horn next to it. "And this one has a cough."

He chuckled. "I did not know that," he said. "Have you tried everything?"

"Um, what's this?" Judy asked, pointing to a big round rubber disk that looked like a target.

"That is a practice pad for the drums."

Drums! *Ba-dum-pum!* Judy liked the sound of that. "Really?"

Mr. Nulty nodded and held out a pair of drumsticks.

Frank bounced on his toes. Judy picked up the drumsticks. Mr. Nulty showed her how to hold them. She heard a beat in her head. "And a one, and a two, and a three . . . " She pounded out a beat. *Ba-da-bum, ba-da-bum, ba-da-bum-bum-bum. Rappa-tap, rappa-tap-tap-tap.*

At last, she had made a sound. A for-real musical beat. No spit came out. And it did not sound like a squeaky mouse or a grumpy parrot.

Judy gave a thumbs-up to drums. "Check me out!" said Judy.

"You're a drummer," said Mr. Nulty.

"Drumroll, please," said Frank. *Ba-dum-bum-CHING!*

Judy Moody was a hip cat. Judy Moody was a cool cat. Judy Moody was her own one-man band. One-*girl* band.

Mr. Nulty had let Judy borrow a pair of drumsticks. She drummed down the hallway. *Ba-dee-da-da.* She drummed on Frank's backpack. *Badda-bo-bee.*

Once Judy started, she couldn't stop drumming. She drummed on the backseat of the Pearls' car all the way home.

She drummed on the door to Stink's room. Stink came out holding his ears. "What's with the drumsticks?" Stink asked.

"I'm a drummer now," said Judy. "It's my thing. It's my *scene.*"

"Do Mom and Dad know?" Stink asked. Judy shook her head no.

"Judy's drumming on the cat!" Stink yelled for Mom and Dad to hear.

"Stink, don't be jive. Being uncool is so fin. As in lame-o."

Stink raced downstairs to tell Mom and Dad. Judy followed. She drummed on the kitchen table. Judy drummed on the cereal box. Judy drummed on the cookie jar.

"What's this all about?" asked Dad.

"New thing," said Judy. "For my bucket list. I tried all the instruments at school, and Mr. Nulty says I'm a drummer."

Judy drummed on the cookie sheet. She drummed on the dishwasher.

"I'll take that," said Mom, whisking away the lid to the spaghetti pot.

"I'm gonna polish with my deck sticks, hitting the skins," Judy told them.

Stink covered his ears. "Make her stop. I'm going bongos."

"Bongos. Ha! That's a drum. Good one, Stink."

"I mean *bonkers*. Why are you talking funny, too?"

"Mr. Nulty let me read his hip cat dictionary," said Judy, grinning.

"I was a little bit bossa nova myself," said Dad. "Back in my middle-school days. Yep. I played drums in a band. Tom Turkey and the Electric Drumsticks."

Mom laughed. "Were you Tom Turkey?"

"Nope," said Dad. "I was lead Electric Drumstick." Everybody cracked up.

Dad took up Judy's drumsticks and showed her a few licks on the kitchen table. Stink got into the jam with a pair of chopsticks. They hit the skins, feeling the rhythm and groovin' to the beat, until Mom clanged the cymbals (pot lids), signaling that it was time to shut 'er down and slap on the hogs.

Ba-dee-do-dum. Pum-pum.

Bucket-List Buddies

On Friday after school, Judy was just about to cross off *Learn a musical instrument* from her list *in pen* when Stink said, "Stop! You can't actually cross that one off."

"Why not?"

"Because no way is the kitchen table an instrument."

ROAR!

Was Stink right? It was true-not-false that she *had not/hadn't* played an actual drum. But if she couldn't cross this one off, her kick-the-bucket list was a big fat flop so far. "I'm calling Grandma Lou," she told him.

Judy told Grandma Lou all about her list. Even though she had gotten triple stickers on her homework, learning to cartwheel was a bust, she was nowhere near going to Antarctica, and she hadn't *actually* played a drum.

Grandma Lou reminded Judy that a bucket list takes time. "I'm helping to raise money for books at the library. They lost a lot of kids' books when the library flooded during the hurricane. I've

been working on it for a long time, but we haven't reached our goal yet. So don't give up, Jelly Bean. I bet you'll be playing a real drum in no time."

"Don't give up. Got it," said Judy.

"The thing about a bucket list is . . . getting there is half the fun. It's not just about crossing things off the list."

"Have fun. Got it," said Judy.

"Tell you what," said Grandma Lou. "There's a dude ranch not far from where I live. Why don't I pick you up Saturday and take you there for a horseback ride?"

"Saturday? As in the day after today? As in tomorrow?"

"As in tomorrow."

Judy put down the phone and tried

to cartwheel through the house. *Wheee . . . oops! Plop.* Rats! It was more like an *un*cartwheel.

Judy told Mom and Dad about the dude ranch. Bad move. Stink wanted to go, too.

Judy tried to protest. "But it's for *my* kick-the-bucket list."

"So?" said Stink. "Who wouldn't want to go to a dude ranch and dress up in cowboy boots and a ten-gallon hat and . . . Grandma Lou's my grandma, too."

It was no use. Stink called Grandma Lou and before you could say horse feathers, Stink was going, too.

Once they got upstairs, Judy said,

"Listen, Stinkerbell, since you're coming to Grandma Lou's, you have to call me Queen Judy all weekend."

"Not!" said Stink.

"Then I bet you five dollars toward my Antarctica trip that I can get you to call me *Queen Judy* three times before the weekend is up. Starting right now."

"No way am I *ever* calling you Queen Judy!"

"That's *one*," said Judy, grinning. "You already owe me one dollar and sixty-six cents."

❧   ❧   ❧

Saturday at last! Dude Ranch Day. Ride-a-Horse and Kick-the-Bucket-List Day.

All morning, Stink galloped around on

a broom and made annoying giddy-up noises. Judy snorted. "I'm the one riding a horse, Stink. You'll be riding a puny pony. You have to be at least four feet tall to ride a real horse. "

"Says who?"

"Says the brochure." Judy waved a pamphlet at him. "Mom found this in the kitchen drawer."

Stink galloped over to her. Judy held it high in the air so Stink could not reach it. He jumped up. He jumped up again.

"Sorry, Shortypants," said Judy.

Toot-a-loo! Judy heard a car horn. "Grandma Lou's here!" She grabbed her stuff and yelled, "I call shotgun!"

"No fair," said Stink. "You have to be outside to call shotgun."

Judy ran out the door. "Shotgun!" she called again.

Stink ran past her and slapped his hand against the door handle of Grandma Lou's Mini. "Shotgun! Actually, it's who-ever touches the car-door handle first."

"But you don't have your shoes on. So *actually*—you have to go back inside. I win." She pulled up the car-door handle just as Grandma Lou was unlocking it. The door *would not/wouldn't* open.

"Ha-ha. Shotgun Suicide!" said Stink, cracking up. "I win!"

"Who died and made you Quick Draw McGraw, Stink?" said Judy.

"Who died and made you queen, Judy?"

"Ha! You just said Queen Judy. That's two. Now you owe me three dollars and thirty-two cents. Sweet!"

Grandma Lou rolled down the window. "Nobody's riding shotgun. Sorry, kiddos. Backseat for both of you."

"I call right side!" said Judy.

"No fairsies," said Stink.

"Stink, you like the left. Left is for lefties," said Grandma Lou.

"Oh yeah," said Stink. "I do like the left. Wait!" He dashed into the house and came back with two pet carrying cases. He buckled himself in. "Phew. I almost forgot Toady and Astro!"

"Stink, why did you have to bring—"

Grandma Lou turned around. "Before we start, let's talk about some rules for the day."

Grandma Lou said no fighting. Grandma Lou said no picking on each other in the car. Grandma Lou said they had to show her that they could get along if they wanted to go to the dude ranch. She promised it was going to be fun.

Judy stared out the window. *If only Stink was not/wasn't being a fun sponge.*

Stink had his nose in the brochure all the way to the dude ranch. He could not stop yak-yak-yakking. "Did you know they have hayrides? Can we go on a hayride?"

"Grandma Lou—" Judy started.

"Maybe I'll be a sheriff. No, a cowboy. No, a sheriff."

"Guess what, Grandma Lou," said Judy.

"And get this," said Stink. "They have archery. Can we shoot a bow and arrow?"

"Grandma Lou, guess what," Judy tried again. "After I—"

"Says here they have a FREE airport shuttle and Swiss mattresses. Whatever that means," said Stink.

Boy howdy! Judy *was not/wasn't* happy about Stinkerbell coming along. She *did not/didn't* want to be in the backseat with him. And now they had to stop at Grandma Lou's to drop off his pets.

Judy closed her eyes and thought about horses. She might be feeling down, but soon she'd be saddling up. She was chomping at the bit to ride a horse. If she ever got out of the car, that is!

"Grandma Lou," said Judy, "after I ride a horse I can cross it off my list. But I promise to have fun first."

Judy pictured a beautiful black stallion

with a mane so shiny it was almost blue.
She imagined bouncing and riding atop
a horse like Black Beauty, running wild,
running free. She could almost feel the
wind in her hair.

Poetry in motion, just like the brochure
said.

"They even have porch rockers for you, Grandma Lou," Stink teased.

"No porch rocking for this granny," said Grandma Lou. "I brought Gertrude." She stuck her hand out the window and patted the red kayak on the car roof. "I'll be row-row-rowing my boat gently down the stream while you cowpokes are eating desert dust."

The Dud Ranch

Yippee-ki-yay! At last, they were out of the hot car. At last, they were at the Majestik— a for-real-and-absolute-positive dude ranch.

"Hey, Judy," said Stink. "Let's pretend it's the O.K. Corral."

"Okay," said Judy. "I'll be Doc Holliday and you can be Wyatt Twerp."

"Hardee-har-har," said Stink. "Never mind. I'll be Wild Bill Hiccup and you can be Calamity Judy."

Judy and Stink took one look around. All they saw was dust. Dust, dust, and more dust. And dirt. And mud. The smell of hay tickled Judy's nose.

Stink pointed to an old Conestoga wagon with a ripped-up canvas and busted wheels. Rusted trucks and tractors collected behind a falling-down silo. "Are you sure this is it?" He held up the brochure to compare. It showed a herd of horses running wild against a blue sky. "It sure doesn't look like the picture."

"This is it!" said Grandma Lou, pointing to the sign over the entrance.

But instead of the Majestik, all it said was MAJEST.

"Ick," said Judy. "They forgot the *I-K*."

"Not so majestic, is it?" said Grandma Lou. "I think maybe this place has seen better days."

Hundreds of noisy black starlings and grackles lined fences, tree branches, and telephone wires, cawing and cackling up a storm. Stink covered his ears. "What is this, a bird farm? It's so loud."

"Who cares," said Judy, playing keep-away with a bad mood. "All that matters is that I get to ride a horse, right, Grandma Lou? Let's head to the stables."

They walked under a giant *M* at the entrance to the ranch and down a dirt path, past a swimming pool that was green with leaves and gunk.

"P.U. Hold your nose," said Stink.

It was hot, and there were piles of horse poop everywhere. And where there was poop, there were flies. Tons of flies. Big fat horseflies buzzed Stink's head. Judy swatted one that landed in her hair.

"You could make a million dollars as a Pooper Scooper here," said Stink.

"Here's the horse poop, but where are the horses?" Judy asked. "I don't see any horses."

"And where are all the dudes?" Stink asked. "This is a dude ranch, right?"

"They should call it a dud ranch," said Judy.

Grandma Lou couldn't help chuckling. "Look, kids, we don't have to stay—"

"But we came to ride a horse," said Judy. "I can't leave until I ride a horse!"

When they got to the stables, two cowhands in jeans, plaid shirts, and cowboy boots told Grandma Lou they'd take care of her young riders.

"Okay, kiddos. Sounds like you're in good hands. I have to go pay at the office, but I'll be back to check on you." Grandma Lou headed for the office in the barn.

"I'm Whip," said one of the cowhands. "Whip Watson. And my buddy here is Lash LaRue."

"Whip and Lash?" said Judy. "Oh,

whiplash! Get it, Stink? Together *they are/they're* WhipLash."

"Smart kid," said Whip, pointing to his brain.

"Yeah, we, um, never heard that one before," said Lash. He and Whip exchanged a look.

"So you want to ride, eh?" asked Whip. "We'll have you two in apple-pie order in no time."

"You buckaroos got here just in time," said Lash. "We have two animals left that aren't out on the trail." He checked his clipboard. "Looks like Tumbleweed and Tamale are still available."

Tumbleweed and Tamale! Lame-o! "Don't you have any horses named Stormy or Shadowboxer?" Judy asked. "Or Diablo?"

"Or Lightning or Thunderbolt?" asked Stink.

Stink climbed up on the bottom rung of the gate and peered into the paddock at the two animals. "I call the horse!" said Stink.

"What do you mean?" Judy asked, rushing over to peer into the stalls. "Aren't they both horses?" All Judy could see of one horse was a black tail. The other looked more like some kind of donkey.

Stink pointed to a sign over the first stall. HI. I'M TAMALE. I'M A HINNY! "That one's a hiney," said Stink. "No *way* am I riding anything called a hiney."

"Stink, stop saying *hiney*," Judy told him, flushing red.

"Cowgirl's right," said Lash LaRue, leading the hinny/hiney over on a pink rope. "This here's what you call a hinny. A hinny is half horse and half donkey."

"He looks like Eeyore," said Stink. "Hee-haw!" The hinny whinnied and kicked up his hiney. Stink jumped out of the way.

Judy tugged at Stink's sleeve, pulling him aside. She took out her bucket list and unfolded it. "Stink. You gotta let me ride the horse. See what it says right here on my list? It says *Ride a horse*. It *does not/ doesn't* say *Ride a hinny.*

"Second of all, you aren't even supposed to be here. This was supposed to be my thing with Grandma Lou. And don't forget you're a shrimpy pants. You have to be four feet tall to ride the horse anyway."

"Shh! I'm only a few inches short." Stink turned to Whip and Lash. "Got any ten-gallon hats around here?"

"Nope, but you can borrow my hat," said Whip, pulling it off his head and

dropping it onto Stink's head.
"Now you're looking real cow-
boy."

Stink tugged on the brim
of his hat and turned to Judy. "Fine. I'll
ride the hinny. Just don't tell anyone."

"I won't tell anyone you rode a hiney,"
said Judy. "Now vamoose!"

Whip led Stink over to the next corral.
At last, it was time to ride! She turned to
Lash LaRue. "Let's hit the trail!" she said.

"Slow down there, Missy. Have you
ridden a horse before?"

"Well, um . . . not unless the horses
on the merry-go-round at the state fair
count."

"Here's the thing," said Lash. "Since

it's your first time, we'll just take a trot around the corral."

Judy could not wait to meet Tumbleweed. Would it be an Arabian with a shiny black mane and braided tail? Or a dappled Appaloosa with a white star on its forehead? She could already hear the *clip-clop* of its hooves and the *jingle-jangle* of its harness.

Lash LaRue came out leading a horse by its bridle. Judy could not believe her eyes! This horse was tall! This horse was high up! This horse was . . . *old!*

This horse was not an Arabian. This horse was not an Appaloosa. This horse was a dusty brown nag with a saggy

middle and gray hair around its eyes and muzzle. The horse's skin hung loose, and it had two long front teeth.

Judy's heart sank like a crashed cartwheel. *Plop.*

At least it was a horse. She'd finally get to ride and cross that off her list.

Lash LaRue helped Judy climb up into the saddle. She put her left foot in the stirrup, grabbed the saddle horn, and swung her right leg up and over the old horse.

Judy was sitting tall in the saddle. The air smelled cleaner up here. The loud racket of the birds faded. She could almost hear the wind roaring in her ears.

Tumbleweed nickered.

"Giddy up, horsey!" Judy called. "Yippee-ki-yay! Ride 'em, cowgirl." But the horse would not budge. Not one *clip*. Not one *clop*.

"Are you sure this horse isn't dead?" Judy asked.

"It's this heat," said Lash. "This old nag ain't what she used to be."

At last, Tumbleweed trotted a few steps. Stopped. Trotted a few more. Stopped again.

This horse did not have the spirit of Black Beauty. This horse was not flying with the wind in its mane. This horse was more glue than gallop.

No way was this the O.K. Corral. Judy had landed smack-dab in the middle of the NOT-O.K. Corral.

Atop the old nag, Judy started to melt in the heat. The smell of horse plop made her feel queasy. She was too hot to swat away flies.

Tumbleweed was slower than a snail in molasses. At this pace, Judy could barely keep her eyes open. Halfway around the

ring, her head flopped and she nodded off to . . .

Sleep? Judy's head jerked back up. Did she really and truly *fall asleep* in the saddle?

She raised herself up in the stirrups and stretched to look over at her brother in the next pen. Stink held the reins of the hinny in one hand and waved his cowboy hat around in the other.

"Yee-haw!" Stink yelled. He boinged and bounced like a rough rider on a mountain trail. He whooped and hollered like a rodeo star at the state fair.

Wild Bill Hiccup was having the ride of his life, while Calamity Judy was Queen of the Dud Ranch.

When Judy and Tumbleweed finally made it around the corral two times, Judy dismounted. She ran over to Stink's corral. "Time to switch, Stink," she called out. "You get to ride the horse now."

"No thanks," Stink yelled as the hinny shook its head and neighed. "Tamale doesn't want to stop yet."

"But it's your turn," said Judy. "It's only fair that you get a turn on the horse."

"I'm good," said Stink.

"Stink, I'll forget about the three dollars and thirty-two cents you owe me if you let me ride that hinny."

"Deal," said Stink.

In no time, Judy found herself atop the hinny and on top of the world! Judy and Tamale trotted and cantered and galloped like a real cowgirl and her trusty sidekick. They rode like the wind. *Poetry in motion!*

What a ride! When she got down, she was dizzy and out of breath.

"How was it?" asked Whip and Lash.

"Great!" said Judy. "That half a horse practically gave me whiplash. For real."

"Glad to oblige, ma'am," said Lash, tipping his hat to Judy.

Just then, Grandma Lou came up and called over the fence. "The stream was too low for kayaking, so I went to the coffee shop." She held up a cow pie in each hand. Ice cream, that is.

"Race ya, Stink!" They ran across the

paddock to Grandma Lou. Judy told all about Tumbleweed and falling asleep and WhipLash and riding a hiney/hinny. "And that's the true story of how I came to ride half a horse," said Judy.

"Sounds like you had a good time," said Grandma Lou.

Drip, drip, drip. Judy licked the ice cream running down her arm. The dude ranch *was not/wasn't* a dud ranch after all!

HypnoToady

On the way back from the dude ranch, Judy, Stink, and Grandma Lou drove past the public library. "Hey, look," said Judy. "They have a giant thermometer like my Antarctica one." At the top it said: SUPPORT YOUR LIBRARY: GO FOR THE GOAL. The red almost reached the top.

"Pretty soon you'll be able to cross that off your list, Grandma Lou," said Judy.

As soon as they reached Grandma Lou's house, Judy erased *Ride a horse* from her kick-the-bucket list and wrote *Ride a hinny*. Then she happily crossed it off.

She held the list up for Grandma Lou to see. "Did you cross anything off your bucket list this week?"

"I did finish *War and Peace* last night," said Grandma Lou.

"Hey! You forgot to cross it off!" said Judy.

"I must have used invisible ink," said Grandma Lou, winking. "Now, you kids go play in the rumpus room until we're ready for spaghetti."

"Let the wild rumpus start!" Stink

called, racing Judy downstairs to the basement. Pugsy pounded down the stairs after them. "So what's next on your basket list?" he asked.

"*Bucket* list, Stink," said Judy.

He pointed to *Face a fear.* "Ooh, let's do this one." He grabbed some scrap paper. "I'll make a list of stuff you're scared of."

- Zombies
  - Bloody Mary, Vampire Squid
    - Blob movies

"That's stuff *you're* scared of, Stink. Here, let me have it." Judy wrote:

- Bees
- Tsunamis
- Blood
- Getting hypnotized
- Sun burning out

Stink added *Ghost in the junk room* to the bottom of her list.

Judy's eyes darted over to the door of the junk room. "For your information, Stink, I'm not afraid of the junk room."

"Ya-huh," said Stink. "Remember last time we were here? You went into the junk room to find Park and Shop, that old board game?"

"Yeah. So?"

"You said you saw a ghost! You ran screaming out of there and we had to push the Ping-Pong table up against the door."

"Okay, okay! So I'm afraid of the junk room! But I'm never-not-ever going in there, so you can forget it."

Stink went down the list. "Bees?"

Judy shivered. "They sting!"

"Tsunami?"

"How am I going to face a tsunami, Stink?"

"Um, you stand in the bathtub and I make really big waves?"

"I'm not afraid of a *bathtub* tsunami, Stink."

"Blood?" Stink asked. "Wait. How are

you going to be a doctor if you're afraid of blood?"

Judy shrugged. "That's why I have to face my fear, Stink."

"Don't look at me. I'm not doing any bleeding, that's for sure. Next."

"Hypnotized. I'm afraid of being hypnotized against my will."

"For real?"

"It's your fault, Stink. You're always watching that toad with the googly eyes on the computer."

"HypnoToad? You're afraid of a cartoon?"

"Whenever anybody stares into his cuckoo-crazy eyes, they go bonkers and have to do whatever he commands."

"I've got it! *I'll* hypnotize you. Then you'll have faced a fear and you can cross it off your list."

"I guess. While you're at it, Stink, can you make me good at contractions? And maybe cartwheels, too?"

Stink ran upstairs and came back with Toady. "Meet HypnoToady!"

"No way!" said Judy, holding her arm out like a stop sign. "Not the toad!"

"What's the matter?" Stink teased. "Are you scared?"

"Yes!" Judy held Pugsy close.

Stink held Toady out in front of Judy. "Ju-dy. Look into my eyes," Stink said. "I'm HypnoToady. You are getting sleepy."

Judy blinked once, twice. "Am I hypnotized yet?" she asked.

"Not yet," said Stink. "Your eyes are getting heavy."

"Pugsy's eyes are getting heavy," said Judy. "I think *he's* hypnotized!"

"Your head feels like a bowling ball," Stink continued. "Your eyelids are melting down your face."

"Gross!" Judy wriggled like a cater-pillar. It was hard to look at Toady.

"Stare into my eyes," said Stink-as-HypnoToady. "Take a deep breath." *Stink* was getting sleepy now. He shook himself awake. "Pretend you are walking into a room full of jawbreakers."

Judy perked up. "Jawbreakers?"

"No talking," said Stink. "Take five deep breaths. Pretend you are going down stairs, lots and lots of stairs, and walk into a room full of mood pillows."

Judy did feel a little sleepy.

"I am HypnoToady. Soon you will be under my spell. You will do as I say. You will not be afraid. Repeat after me. 'I will not be afraid.'"

"I will not be afraid," said Judy.

"HypnoToady says 'Stand up,'" said Stink.

Judy stood up!

"HypnoToady says 'Do five jumping jacks,'" Stink commanded.

Judy jumped up and scissored her arms five times. Stink's eyes almost bugged out of his head.

"HypnoToady says 'Act like a zombie,'" commanded Stink.

Judy stuck her arms out in front of her. She walked stiffly around the room, moaning and groaning, muttering, "Brains. Me want brains."

"It's working," said Stink, in a voice barely above a whisper. "It's really

working!" Suddenly, Stink had an idea. A brilliant, for-real, face-your-fears idea.

"Walk over to the junk room," he said. Judy zombie-walked to the junk room.

"HypnoToady commands you—put your hand on the doorknob," said Stink. Something was not right. Judy did not put her hand on the doorknob. Something was wrong. The spell was wearing off!

"HypnoToady commands you—open the door," Stink tried.

Judy's hand reached for the doorknob. Was her hand shaking? She opened the door a crack. A gust of cold air whooshed out. The junk room was dark.

"HypnoToady commands you—enter the junk room!"

Judy *could not/couldn't* stand it for one more second. "No way, no how. Forget it. Nuh-uh. I'm SO not going in there, Stinkerbell."

"Wait. I thought you were . . . but . . . aren't you . . . hypnotized?"

"Not even. Did you really think . . . ?" Judy cracked up. "I was so faking."

Just then, they heard a strange noise coming from inside the junk room.

Aieee! A moaning? A groaning? A sighing? A crying? Stink gave Judy a push—right into the junk room!

"Hey!" Judy blinked, trying to see in the dark. She felt along the wall for a light switch, but couldn't find one.

Judy took a deep breath. She took one step into the junk room. And another. A crack of milky light shone through a cobwebby window. Under that window, huddled in the corner, was a shapeless white . . .

"GHOST!" Judy screamed. "Run for your life!" She ran out of the room and up the stairs, Stink and Pugsy at her heels. Grandma Lou looked at their white-as-a-sheet faces. "You two look like you've just seen a ghost!"

"That's because *we d-d-did*!" said Stink, sputtering and trying to spit out the words.

"*I* did," said Judy. "There's a g-g-ghost in your junk room, Grandma Lou. No lie!"

Grandma Lou let out a breath. "So Otis must be back."

Judy looked at Stink. Stink looked at Judy. "Otis?" they said at the same time.

"My ghost. He prefers to be called the Virginia Beach Strangler, but I call him Otis. Comes back to the junk room every year. He likes to hang out by the water heater where it's warm."

Stink's eyes grew as big as jumbo gum-balls.

"You're just faking us out, right, Grandma Lou?" Judy asked. "Like the time we pranked you and pretended a ghost named Bob was in my room?"

"I'll never tell," said Grandma Lou with a twinkle in her eye.

Whether or not it was Otis, Judy had seen *something* in the junk room. "C'mon, Stink," said Judy, dragging him back downstairs.

"You're not really going back in there, are you?" Stink asked.

"I have to face my fear sometime. Otherwise I'll never finish my bucket list. And I have to finish it before the fourth grade."

Outside the junk room, Judy grabbed a tennis racket. She raised the racket and stepped inside. She took one tiny step, then another. *AAGH!* Something touched her hair! Something tickled her ear. A long finger reached out and wrapped itself around her neck.

"Help!" Judy screamed. "It's Otis! He got me!" She pulled at the tentacle around her neck and . . .

Click! The light came on! Otis the ghost, aka the Virginia Beach Strangler, was just the old pull-cord for the light.

The dim bulb cast spooky shadows on the wall.

"You can come in now, Stink."

Stink tiptoed in and grabbed hold of Judy's hand. She did not push it away.

They saw board games and beach chairs and basketballs. Rolled-up rugs and ropes and Christmas wreaths. The water heater gurgled and burbled. Wind whistled through a duct-taped window.

"There he is!" cried Stink.

Judy whipped around, dropping the tennis racket on the floor. "There *who* is?"

"Otis!" cried Stink, pointing to a shapeless white lump in the corner.

Judy let go of Stink's hand. She inched forward, one step at a time. She could hear her own heartbeat pounding like a drum, *ba-dum, ba-dum.* "*Face my fear, face my fear, face my fear,*" she whispered to herself.

There, in the deepest, darkest corner of the junk room, huddled Otis, the ghost! And Otis was . . . a dusty old white sheet?

The dusty old white sheet was draped

over something bumpy and lumpy. Judy
reached down and yanked off the sheet.
The lumpy bump was not Otis. The
lumpy bump was not a ghost. It was a
glittery, shiny, silvery . . . drum set!

Beneath the sheet was a snare drum, a bass drum, and a tom-tom, plus a hi-hat and cymbals. The bass drum said TOM TURKEY AND THE ELECTRIC DRUMSTICKS.

"Here's your ghost, Stink!" said Judy.

"The ghost is Dad's old drum set?" Stink asked.

Judy cracked up. "Say hi to Otis." She slid in behind the bass drum and sat down on the small stool. She blew dust off the top of the snare drum.

Judy lined up her feet on the kick pedals.

She closed her eyes and took a deep breath, until she heard the heartbeat of a rhythm in her head.

She opened her eyes and picked up the drumsticks.

Ba-da-da-dum-dum-dum-de-dum.

Pshhhh! Ride that cymbal!

Do Not/Don't-Kick-the-Bucket List

The very next weekend, Judy tried one more time to turn a cartwheel down the front hall. *Yipes!* Her pants fell down. She tried again. *Crash!* She knocked over the coat tree.

"Judy! Take it outside!" Dad called.

Judy went outside and tumbled in the grass. She ended up in a tangle of arms and legs like a pretzel.

Grandma Lou beeped and pulled up

in her yellow Mini. Judy ran over to the window. "Want to know the secret to a cartwheel?" Grandma Lou asked. "You have to let your mind go. Take it from the 1959 YMCA Newcomer Gymnast of the Year."

"You were?" Just then, Judy noticed that the car was filled to the gills with heaps of stuff covered in old sheets.

"Did you bring Otis the ghost with you or something?" Judy asked.

"Wait and see," said Grandma Lou. Mom, Dad, and Stink came out into the driveway. Grandma Lou opened the hatchback. "Ta-da!"

"Dad's old drum set? For me?" Judy asked.

"Your dad and I talked it over. These are yours now, Jelly Bean. Keep marching to the beat of your own drum."

Dad handed her a brand-new pair of drumsticks. "Tom Turkey and the Electric Drumsticks must live on."

"You can be Tammy Turkey," said Stink.

Judy cracked up. "Wow! Thanks!" She hugged her dad.

"This'll be fun," said Dad. "I'm rusty, but I can teach you a few things. Maybe a paradiddle and a drumroll and—"

"Can I be a drum bum, too?" Stink asked. Mom and Dad set the drums in the driveway, and Judy beat out a rhythm with Dad to his old favorite—the Mashed Potato. Stink crashed the cymbal.

Half the neighborhood came out when they heard the racket. Rocky and Frank tapped on their knees like bongos. Grandma Lou and Mrs. Soso danced the Mashed Potato. Even Izzy Azumi, Future Dog Owner, grooved to the beat along with her father and brother. Dad took off on the snare, playing several licks in a row.

"Tom Turkey lives!" yelled Stink.

"We're heating up the whole neighborhood with these tubs and pies!" said Judy. "That's hepcat talk for drums and cymbals."

Plip. Plip, plip. Plop. Oh, no! Judy started to feel drops.

"I hate to end this jam session," said Mom, "but it's starting to rain. Let's get all you drum bums inside."

After they got the drums into the garage, Judy said to Grandma Lou, "Let's compare our kick-the-bucket lists."

She snuggled up next to her bucket-list buddy on the couch. Just the two of them. Judy crossed off *Learn a musical instrument.* "Look how many cross-offs I have! Have you crossed anything off your list lately?"

"I finally learned to dance the rumba," said Grandma Lou. "And I'm taking a sign language class." She showed Judy the sign for *bucket list.* She showed Judy the signs for *Grandma Lou, Judy,* and *I love you.*

"I have an idea," said Judy. "The house across the street from you has a bouncy castle. Maybe you could ask them if you can camp out there. That way, you could cross off *Sleep in a castle.*"

"Not exactly the castle I was hoping for," Grandma Lou said, chuckling.

"What about the books for the library?" Judy asked. You'll be able to cross that one off soon, right?" She looked the list up and down. "Hey! That one's not even on your list."

"Sure it is," said Grandma Lou. "See where it says *Make a difference?* I didn't want everything on my bucket list to be about me, me, me. So I thought helping kids to read is a good way to help others. It's about opening your heart and thinking about somebody in need."

Judy looked at her own list with new eyes. She *had not/hadn't* thought about helping others. She had only thought of herself. Judy chewed on the end of her Grouchy pencil.

I want to make a difference, too. Judy thought about how much *she* loved to read. Suddenly, she felt sad for all those kids who didn't have books to read because of the flood.

Maybe she could give some of her books to the library. Some of her fifty-six classic Nancy Drew mysteries. But a lot of those books were Mom's from when she was a girl.

Lightbulb! She had an even better idea. A triple-trifecta, awesome-sauce-sticker idea. She, Judy Moody, would open her heart *and* her piggy bank.

Judy ran upstairs and came back with her piggy bank. *Ka-ching!* She shook it loudly so Grandma Lou could hear the rattle of all the money in there.

"Grandma Lou," said Judy, "I want you to have this."

"Isn't that your Going-to-Antarctica money?"

"Yep! But I want it to help those kids who need books at the library. My poop-scooping money's in here, and my allowance. Plus the dollar I got from Stink and some quarters I found in the couch cushions. Also nickels from my gumball machine and half my lucky penny jar."

"That's your life savings, Jelly Bean. I wouldn't feel right taking this."

"It's okay. I can save up again. I know I can. I can poop scoop and not spend my allowance and trick Stink into giving me some. Who knows, I might even start a band and put out a tip jar."

"Are you sure about this?"

"Don't worry. I have tons of time before fourth grade to save for Antarctica."

"I don't know what to say, Judy. You sure have a big heart. This will really help with books for the library." Grandma Lou touched her chin to sign *Thank you* and held up her thumb and index and pinky fingers to make the *I love you* sign to Judy.

Grandma Lou gave Judy a hug and a squeeze. "I think this calls for a cup of cocoa," she said, heading for the kitchen. She folded her bucket list and tucked it inside her purse.

Suddenly it hit Judy.

Before she knew it, Grandma Lou would be D-O-N-E *done* with her bucket list. If she was done with her list, did that mean . . . ?

Judy *could not/couldn't* think the thought.

She listened for the kettle. It wasn't whistling yet. She had time. Judy glanced around to make sure there were no spying eyes in sight. Then she lifted the bucket list from out of Grandma Lou's purse.

Judy took out a pen and added new things to Grandma Lou's list:

New Additions!
☐ Read all 7 Harry Potters
☐ AND MOBY-DICK
☐ Go Glow-in-the-Dark BOWLING
☐ Take Ballroom lessons
☐ Learn to surf
☐ Learn to play ukulele
☐ Build a birdhouse
☐ Take Judy to ride London Eye
☐ Climb K-2 (2nd highest mountain ever) AND EIFFEL TOWER

There. That should take a good long while. Grandma Lou's bucket list was now a rain-barrel list. A bathtub list! Judy wanted to make double-triple-extra sure that Grandma Lou would be around for a good long time.

She, Judy Moody, was in a mood. A good mood. A twirl-in-the-air cartwheel mood.

Judy closed her eyes and pictured what Izzy Azumi, Future Dog Owner, had shown her: *H.H.F.F. Hand, hand, foot, foot.* She remembered the secret Grandma Lou had shared with her: *Let your mind go.*

Judy Moody stretched her arms over her head. She drew in a deep breath. One, two, three . . . she took a running start and let her mind go.

Over she went—hand, hand, foot, foot.

She did it! No plunk. No plop. No
pretzel. She, Judy Moody, had twirled
through the air, whirled through the air,
and landed on her own two feet.

Judy cartwheeled across the front
yard. She cartwheeled along the side of
the house. She cartwheeled past the old

swing set, past the T.P. Club tent, down to the creek and back again.

Wheee! Her head was spinning. Her world was twirling. But there was no stopping her now.

She couldn't wait to cross that cartwheel off her list.

She, Judy Moody, Inventor of the Porcupainless, had finally done a cartwheel, beaten contractions, ridden a hinny, and faced a fear. She had even made music and made a difference.

There was still more to do — Antarctica, the London Eye, her own newspaper. It was all ahead of her, but she was readier than ever.

She would/she'd march to the beat of her own drum, all the way to fourth grade.

Someday.

Ba-dum-pum. Pshhhh!

Megan McDonald is the author of the popular Judy Moody and Stink series, as well as the Judy Moody and Friends series for new readers. She has written many other books for children, including the Ant and Honey Bee stories, the Sisters Club series, and several picture books. Before she began writing full-time, Megan McDonald worked as a librarian, a bookseller, and a living-history actress. She lives in Northern California with her husband, Richard Haynes, who is also a writer.

Peter H. Reynolds
is the illustrator of the
popular Judy Moody and
Stink series in addition
to many other books,
including several for

which he is also author. They include his
Creatrilogy of picture books: *The Dot, Ish,*
and *Sky Color.* His book *The Dot* has even
inspired International Dot Day, which
is celebrated around the world every
September. Besides writing and illustrating,
Peter H. Reynolds is a bookstore owner,
animator, and educator. He lives in
Massachusetts with his family.

Dear Megan McDonald, would you rather:

Eat the world's largest jawbreaker or a Screamin' Mimi's ice-cream cone?

I think I'm already the proud owner of the World's Largest Jawbreaker, so I'd have to choose a Screamin' Mimi's ice-cream cone. Besides, the real Screamin' Mimi's is in my hometown!

Have a bowl of Mood Flakes or a plate of silver-dollar pancakes for breakfast?

I've got plenty of moods already, so I'm with Stink—silver-dollar pancakes are the best!

Wear a Sybil Ludington costume or a Nancy Drew outfit?

Sybil Ludington, the Revolutionary War hero who rode twice as far as Paul Revere, was a real historical figure. I've always admired her courage and pluck. I'd choose to dress like her any day!

Solve a mystery or solve a math word problem?

My favorite books to read are mysteries, so it's no mystery which I'd choose. I love trying to solve the mystery before the book is over.

Read a book or write a book?

Help! I LOVE BOTH!

Get a for-real glimpse of the Loch Ness monster or of Bigfoot?

Bigfoot! He drives an ice-cream truck, right?

Dear Peter H. Reynolds, would you rather:

Eat a peanut-butter cup or chocolate-covered raisins?

I'd take the chocolate-covered raisins because my twin brother, Paul, loves peanut-butter cups—so I am sure he'd share with me!

Drink a cup of tea or a mug of coffee?

Having grown up in a very British home, I would rather drink tea. I also love painting with tea!

Have a Boston Tub Party or go on a Midnight Zombie Walk?

I grew up and live in the Boston area, so hands down, I'd rather have a Boston Tub Party. In fact, from my studio at FableVision, I have a view of the Boston Tea Party ship.

Take a trip to Argentina or a trip to Antarctica?

I've already been to Argentina a bunch of times. My dad was born there in a town called Tandil. I have been dreaming about visiting Antarctica for a long time. I even have a travel brochure pinned to my Dream Board in my studio, aka the Sanctuary.

Draw a picture of Judy Moody or a picture of Stink?

What a tough choice! It's almost a tie, but I have to say, I am always amazed at how few lines it takes to create Stink. His hair looks like a lawn. I'm going to have to say Stink. (Don't tell Judy!)

Get a for-real glimpse of the Loch Ness monster or of Bigfoot?

Bigfoot scares me. The Loch Ness monster would dip back below the water and I'd be safe on shore—so I choose Nessie.

Take the Personality Quiz!

Are you more like Judy or more like Stink?
Take the test and find out!

If you found a fake hand in the toilet,
you would most likely
> a) laugh your pants off
> b) scream and run

If you couldn't have a two-toed sloth for
a new pet, you would get a
> a) hamburger-eating Venus flytrap
> b) rescued guinea pig

You would rather sleep in a
> a) bunk bed
> b) race car bed

If you were done with your homework,
you would then most likely
> a) make a Me collage
> b) read the *S* encyclopedia

For your school picture, you would
> a) leave your hair wild and messy
> b) spike your hair

The worst smell you can imagine is
    a) smelly sneakers
    b) a corpse flower

If you went on a trip, you would visit
    a) the Wall of (ABC) Gum in California
    b) a Gross-Me-Out exhibit at the museum

If you could join a club, it would be
    a) the My-Name-Is-a-Poem Club
    b) the Short-People-Rule-the-World Club

Your favorite flavor of Screamin' Mimi's ice
cream would probably be
    a) Rain Forest Mist
    b) Coconut Snowstorm

If you chose more a answers than b answers, you are more like Judy. If you chose more b answers than a answers, you are more like Stink. *Same-same!*

If you chose the same number of a and b answers, then you need a math tutor!

BE SURE TO CHECK OUT STINK'S ADVENTURES!

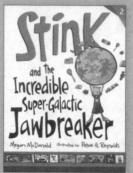

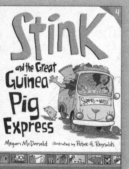

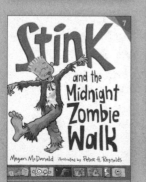

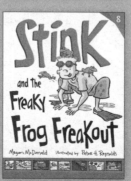

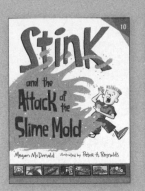

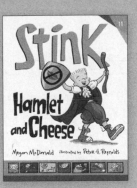

JUMP-START YOUR STINK COLLECTION WITH BOXED SETS — EACH OFFERING A TRIO OF PAPERBACK TITLES:

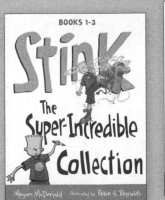

Judy Moody and Stink are starring together!

In full color!

New to the Moody universe?

Try a boxed set of the first three full-color books starring Judy Moody and Stink in paperback!

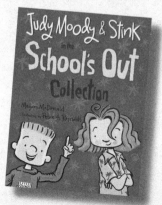